D0944048

JUST SAY PLEASE

BY GINA AND MERCER MAYER

Westport, Connecticut

Copyright © 1993 Mercer Mayer. All rights reserved. Unauthorized reproduction, in any manner, is prohibited.
Published by Reader's Digest Young Families, Inc. Printed in the U.S.A. LITTLE CRITTER® is a registered trademark of
Mercer Mayer. READER'S DIGEST KIDS & DESIGN is a registered trademark of The Reader's Digest Association, Inc.
ISBN: 0-89577-772-X

My teacher said that good manners are
important. She also said that everyone
in our class could use a little help with
good manners.

We made a good manners chart.
We took turns telling the teacher
what to put on it.

I said, "Cover your mouth and
nose when you sneeze."
My dad told me that. The teacher
said that was a very good one.

The class went over everything
on the list, one by one.

Remember to say, "Please."
I remember to say please
when I want to stay up
past my bedtime.

Remember to say, "Thank you."
I always remember to
say thank you when
I get what I want.

Take turns.
I take turns most of the time.
But sometimes it's
so hard to wait.

Don't interrupt when someone is talking.
I guess that's why Mom gets so mad
when I talk to her while
she's on the phone.

Share.
I didn't know *sharing* was good manners. I wonder if my sister knows about that.

If you bump into someone or step on someone's toe, say, "Excuse me."
I guess that keeps people from getting mad at you.

Don't put your elbows
on the table.
I didn't know *elbows*
were bad manners.

Say you're sorry when
you do something wrong.
I'm not too good at that.

Put your napkin
on your lap at
the dinner table.
I thought that was
just so silly.

My teacher said that we would go over the list
every morning so that we could tell her what
we did to show good manners.

I thought that was neat.
I decided to try to have
good manners right away.

When I got home, I ran in the front door and
knocked my sister down. I said, "Excuse me."
That didn't help. She cried anyway.

I went to tell Mom. She was talking
on the phone. I forgot I'm not supposed
to interrupt when someone is talking.
So I said I was sorry.

Boy, was she surprised!
She didn't even get mad at me
for interrupting.

When Dad came home, I asked him to play
a game with me. He said he was too tired.
I said, "Please."
But he still said, "No."
I guess good manners
don't always work.

At dinner I put my napkin on my lap.
My sister asked me why.
I said, "Because it's good manners."

Then my napkin fell on the floor.
My sister said, "You dropped your
good manners."

When Mom passed the rolls, I remembered
to say thank you. Mom said my teacher was doing
a great job teaching us good manners.

I even remembered to keep
my elbows off the table.
Dad didn't, though.

After dinner I let my sister color
my homework picture.
I thought it was nice of me
to share my homework.

The next day at school, we went over the good manners list. We each told how we used good manners.

Only one other critter in my class
had better manners than me.
She got a big sticker that said
I HAVE GOOD MANNERS. It was cool.

I'm working really hard to remember
my good manners because my teacher
gives out a sticker every day.

And I love to get stickers.